THIS BOOK BELONGS TO

....

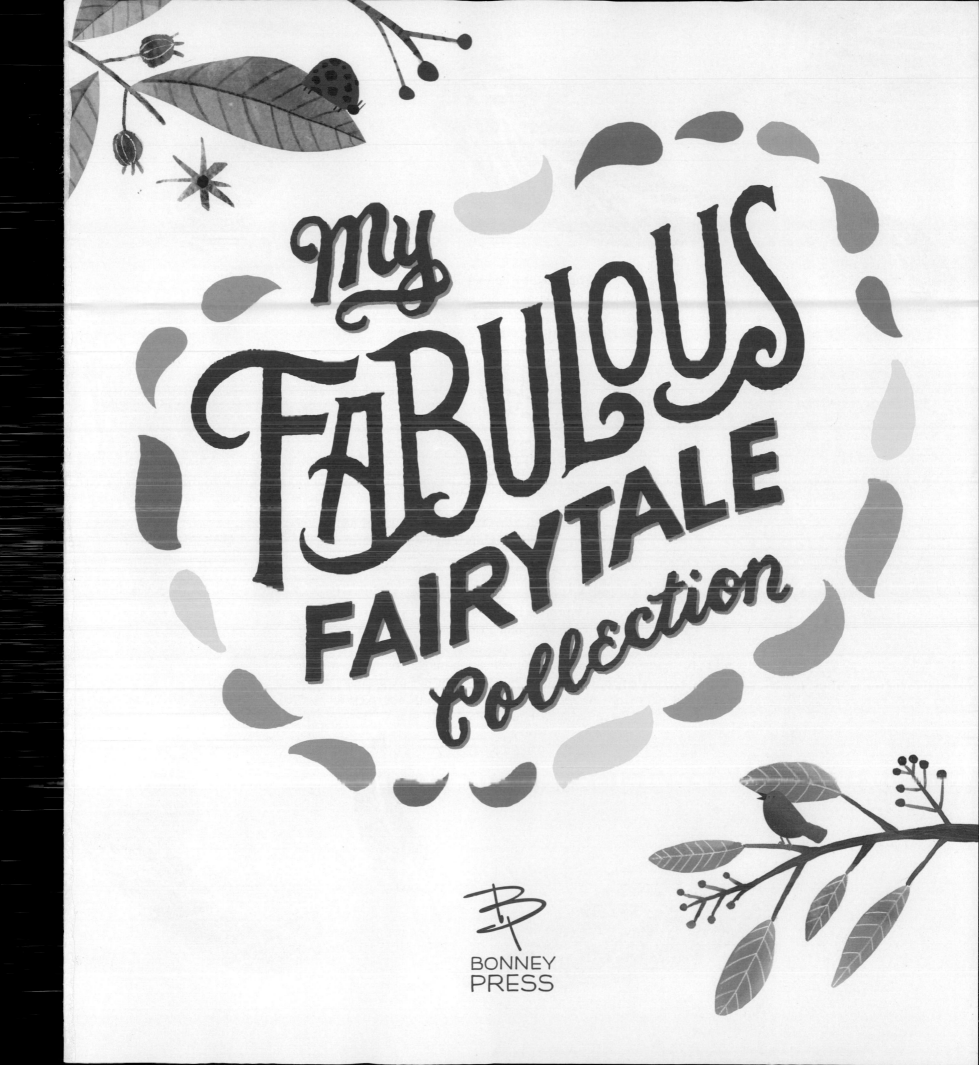

My FABULOUS FAIRYTALE Collection

BONNEY PRESS

Published by Bonney Press,
an imprint of Hinkler Books Pty Ltd 2016
45-55 Fairchild Street
Heatherton Victoria 3202 Australia
www.hinkler.com.au

BONNEY
PRESS

© Hinkler Books Pty Ltd 2016

Illustrators: Agnès Ernoult, Seo Kim, Alida Massari, Rafael Mayani,
Thai My Phuong, Carmen Saldaña.

Text: Katie Hewat
Design: Paul Scott and Pooja Desai
Editorial: Emily Murray
Prepress: Graphic Print Group

ISBN: 978 1 4889 0272 7

Printed and bound in China

CONTENTS

INTRODUCTION

For centuries, fairytales have been shared with children as a way of teaching values, imparting wisdom and demonstrating the strangeness and wonder of the world. The fairytales we know and love today, including those in this collection, have their roots in oral folktale history and the publications of writers and scholars such as the Brothers Grimm, whose final edition of *Kinder- und Hausmärchen* (*Children's and Household Tales*) contained over 200 stories, and Charles Perrault, whose writings helped lay the foundations for the fairytale genre as a whole.

Fairytales appear in every culture around the world, but regardless of their origin, they have always had our shared human experiences at heart – our hopes and fears, our desires and insecurities. They contain vital information about our societies, our histories and ourselves, passed down in oral and written form, developing and evolving with each retelling. The stories that best captured the hearts and minds of their audiences were the ones that were passed on to new audiences, generation after generation.

Sharing fairytales with children at bedtime is a wonderful way to continue this rich, vitally important tradition of storytelling – it connects us with our past and with those who shared these stories before us, while providing the next generation with the means to do the same. We hope that you enjoy this timeless collection of fairytales, with these entertaining adaptations accompanied by stunning illustrations, so that they can form part of your family's history too.

Once upon a time there was a poor young man who owned nothing but...

a *very* clever cat.

One day, as the young man sat eating his poor meal of bread and water, the crafty cat hatched a cunning plan.

'Master,' he said, 'Give me a pair of boots and your bag and I will make all of your dreams come true.'

Now the young man, being entirely without imagination, thought his cat was referring to his lifelong dream of eating a whole goose in one sitting.

So with his last few coins, the young man bought the cat a pair
of cat-sized boots and gave him his only bag.

Off went the cat to the field. First, he began by luring a large hare from its warren and sweeping it up in his sack.

Then he swung the sack over his shoulder and began on his way to the royal palace. The cat was very pleased with his perfect plan, and he *whistled* while he walked.

Once the cat arrived at the palace, he was taken before the king who was in the middle of eating his lunch. With a deep bow, the cat presented the hare as a gift, stating that it was from the marvellous Marquis of Carabas.

The king was delighted, as roasted hare was among his favourite meals. He replied excitedly with a jumble of words the cat couldn't understand, as the king was **gobbling** down a giant turkey leg.

Next, the cat used his wiles to catch two big, *juicy* partridges in the cornfield.

Again, the cat *whistled* his way to the palace and made a present of the partridges to the king. 'I say, it has been too long since I've had such a fine meal as these birds will make,' said the king with a satisfied grin.

His majesty was so pleased with his gift that he rewarded the cat with a gold coin. The cat left the palace clutching the coin to his chest and purring with pride.

One day shortly after, the cat learned that the king was to take a carriage ride along the riverside with his beautiful daughter, the princess.

Seeing an opportunity to progress his plan, the cat asked his master to take a bath in the river. While he was bathing, the king's carriage passed by and the cat cried out, 'HELP! The Marquis of Carabas is drowning!'

The king, seeing the faithful cat who had brought him delicious gifts, ordered his guards to stop and help.

The cat hid the young man's rags under a nearby rock and told the king that thieves had stolen his master's clothes. So the king ordered his guard to fetch a fine suit for the Marquis of Carabas to wear.

The young man was very puzzled by what was taking place, but happily accepted the fine clothing and the king's kind invitation to join him and the princess on their drive.

The cat marched on ahead of the carriage until he met some people working in a meadow that was owned by a cruel ogre.

The cat chatted happily with the workers but, before leaving, warned them, 'The king will soon pass by. You must tell him that the Marquis of Carabas owns this land, or the ogre will be **very angry!'** The frightened folk did as they were asked.

'A very fine field indeed!' said the king, as he offered the young man some tea cake.

The cat continued on ahead until he met a farmer who was harvesting corn in another field owned by the ogre.

The cat chatted pleasantly with the friendly farmer before giving him the same warning he had given to the workers.

So when the king passed by, the man told him, 'The Marquis of Carabas owns this corn, Your Majesty.'

The king was very impressed with the handsome marquis and his wealth.

Eventually the cat arrived at the cruel ogre's castle. It was well-known that the ogre had *magical powers*, and the cat was counting on this to complete the final piece of his plan.

'I have been told that you have a gift,' said the cat. 'They tell me that you can change yourself into any creature you choose, such as a lion. **Surely** this cannot be true?'

'It is true! I'll prove it to you,' said the proud ogre, and he turned himself into a **growling** lion.

The cat got such a fright that he tried to scramble up a nearby cupboard, which was rather awkward because of his boots. When he saw the ogre had finally returned to his normal form, he carefully climbed down.

'I'm very impressed!' said the cat. 'But I have also been told that you can change yourself into a small animal, such as a mouse. Surely, though, *that* is impossible?'

'IMPOSSIBLE?' roared the ogre. 'Watch and see!'

The ogre turned into a tiny mouse and began to run around the room. Grinning a mischievous grin, the cat watched the mouse for a few moments, then quickly pounced and ate him up!

When the king's coach arrived outside the castle, the cat said, 'Welcome to the castle of my Lord, the Marquis of Carabas.'

'*What?* My Lord Carabas!' cried the king. 'Does this fine castle belong to you too?' After a quick glance from the cat, the young man agreed that the castle was in fact his own.

The cat then led the marquis and his guests through to the Great Hall where the servants, happy to be rid of the cruel ogre, had laid out a grand feast.

During the meal the young man, with the help of his trusty cat, charmed both the king and the princess, and soon the princess was completely in love.

The king was so impressed by the marquis's riches that he insisted that the marquis marry his daughter the very next day.

They lived *happily ever after*, and the cat became a great lord. He never had to chase mice again; although sometimes he chose to, just for fun!

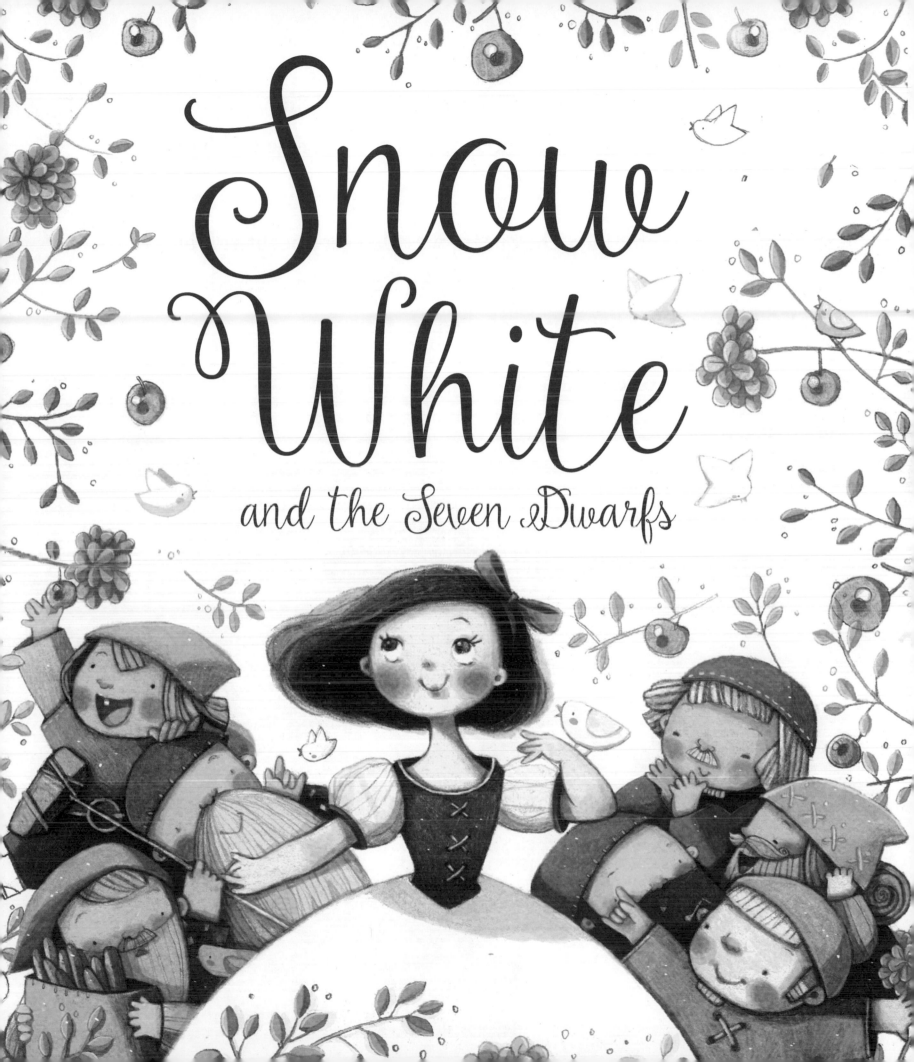

Snow White

and the Seven Dwarfs

Once upon a time there lived a princess named Snow White. She had skin as white as snow, lips as red as a rose and hair as **black** as ebony.

Snow White's stepmother, the queen, was also very beautiful, but very vain. She owned a magic mirror which always answered truthfully to any question it was asked.

The queen would often stand in front of the mirror combing her long hair and ask:

'Mirror, mirror, on the wall, Who is *fairest* of them all?'

And the mirror would sigh, wondering why nobody ever asked questions like, 'What is the meaning of life?' But it would reply,

'You are fairest of all.'

This made the queen *very* happy.

As Snow White grew up, she became even more beautiful. One morning, when the queen asked her question, the mirror replied, a little too cheerfully, *'Snow White is fairest of all.'* The queen flew into a terrible rage and called her trusted huntsman to her.

'I want Snow White *gone*!' she told him. 'Take her into the woods and tie her to a tree. She will be eaten by wild animals and never return.' The huntsman set off to do as he was told.

But when the huntsman took Snow White into the forest, and she happily chatted away and offered to carry his bow for him, he found he could not bring himself to do what the queen had ordered; so he let her go.

'Run away as far as you can, and never return,' he told Snow White. So she ran into the forest, and kept running for as long as she could.

Just as cold and hunger finally
set in, she saw a small cottage
in the distance. Finding nobody
at home, she gently opened the door
and went inside.

Inside the cottage, she found a *tiny* table with seven very small place settings. In the kitchen she found bread and water, which she savoured while sitting in a *tiny* chair.

The cottage was warm and comfortable, and Snow White was very tired, so she curled up on one of the seven *tiny* beds and was soon sleeping soundly.

When it was dark outside, the owners of the cottage came home. They were **seven dwarfs** who mined in the mountains for gold and silver.

The dwarfs carried their candles into the cottage and were very frightened by the **giant** they found asleep inside.

'What *is* it?'

'A monster!'

'What shall we do?'

'Attack it!'

'Wait, wait, wait,' said another. 'It's just a human girl.'

The dwarfs all crowded around Snow White to get a closer look.

'So it is. Silly us!'

Snow White awoke with a start to find seven little men standing around her. She was frightened at first but quickly realised the dwarfs were very friendly.

When Snow White told them her story, they soon became fast friends and the dwarfs decided that she should stay with them in their cottage.

'But you must be very careful,' one of the dwarfs warned her. 'You may still be in danger from the queen. So don't go out into the woods alone and never, ever open the door to a stranger.'

Back at the castle, the queen (believing that Snow White was no longer a problem) arose the next morning, went to her magic mirror and asked:

'Mirror, mirror, on the wall,
Who is *fairest* of them all?'

The mirror replied with a groan,

'Snow White is fairest of all.'

'That foolish huntsman! He can't even be trusted to get rid of a silly little girl! If you want something done right, you have to do it *yourself.*'

So the jealous queen, who was consumed with anger, decided she would not rest until she found where Snow White was hiding.

First, the queen began by plastering 'WANTED' posters in every town and along every roadside. But the creatures of the forest, who loved Snow White, made it their mission to tear each one down. After receiving no news of Snow White's whereabouts, the queen realised the answer had been right in front of her all along.

She stood before her magic mirror and asked:

'Mirror, mirror, oh so *fragile*,
Where has the **brat** been all this while?'

The mirror, feeling somewhat alarmed at the queen's angry tone and her ability to smash him into one hundred tiny pieces, sadly replied,

'Snow White lives with the seven dwarfs in their cottage in the forest.'

The queen set to work on an evil plan. Disguising herself as a peasant woman, she scoured the markets for the **biggest,** *juiciest* apples she could find. Then she selected the best apple of the bunch and carefully brushed one side with poison.

The queen then placed the apples in a basket and made her way to the dwarfs' cottage.

Once there, she waited patiently for the dwarfs to go to work.

'Apples for sale!' called the queen outside the cottage window. Remembering the dwarfs' warning, Snow White cautiously peered out the window, and upon seeing the delicious apples in the basket, said sadly, 'I am not to let anyone in.'

'There is no need,' replied the queen, as she took a large bite from the un-poisoned side of the apple. 'Here, try this,' she said, and passed the apple through the window.

Snow White thought she'd much rather have her own apple rather than a germy, half-eaten one. But not wanting to be rude to the kind old lady, she took the apple and bit into the opposite side. The poison struck immediately and Snow White **fell** to the **floor**.

Delighted at her success, the queen cackled with laughter all the way back the castle.

As soon as she arrived, she went straight to her magic mirror.

This time, in answer to her question, the bored mirror answered,

'You are fairest of all.'

The queen was very pleased.

That evening, the dwarfs found Snow White lying on the cottage floor. Distraught, they tried *everything* they could think of to wake her, but nothing worked.

The dwarfs wanted her to be at peace, so they made Snow White a glass casket and took her into the woods where they could watch over her. Even the animals came to mourn for her.

One day, a *handsome* prince happened by the casket and was instantly mesmerised by the *beautiful* girl inside. He knew he could not live without being able to look upon her lovely face, so he asked the dwarfs for permission to take her back to his kingdom.

The dwarfs agreed, sad to lose Snow White, but glad that she would have a fine resting place.

The prince thanked the dwarfs, and began to ready the casket for the long journey. But as he lifted the casket, the piece of poisoned apple was freed from Snow White's mouth and she **instantly awoke.**

Snow White and the prince fell *madly in love*, and soon travelled to the prince's kingdom to be married.

They lived happily ever after, often returning to the cottage in the forest to visit their favourite friends, the dwarfs.

The queen, having believed this whole time that Snow White was gone, stood in front of her magic mirror one day and asked her favourite question. This time, the mirror gleefully answered:

'Evil queen, who art so vain,
Snow White is alive again.
She is lovely of heart and face,
And has a thousand times
your beauty and grace.'

And with that, the queen exploded in a puff of green, jealousy-filled smoke; never to be seen again.

JACK
AND THE BEANSTALK

Once upon a time there was a boy named Jack who lived in a small cottage with his mother. The only possession they had in the world was a cow named Milky-White, whose milk they sold at the market.

But one day, Milky-White stopped giving milk, and Jack's mother told him to sell her so they could get some money for food.

The next morning, on his way to the market, Jack met a strange old man who proposed a swap: Milky-White for a handful of beans.

'But they're not just any beans,' the man told Jack. *'They're magic!'* Jack knew he had to have them. 'If they don't grow,' the old man said, 'I'll give you your cow back and will throw in a free bag of cow manure for your trouble.' That sealed the deal – they made the exchange.

WHOOP!!!!

Once he was around the next bend, the old man let out a 'whoop!' He couldn't believe his luck. Ever since he'd eaten one of those awful beans he'd had *terrible* pains in his stomach. He'd been coughing up leaves, and shoots had begun growing out of his ears.

When Jack arrived home, he proudly showed his mother the beans
and told her of the special deal he had made with the old man.
His mother took the beans and looked at them.

'WHAT?' she exclaimed. 'How could you be so foolish as to give away our Milky-White for a handful of beans?' And with that, she threw the beans at Jack and they bounced out the window.

To Jack's delight, when he awoke the next morning he saw that the beans had grown in the night. They had formed a beanstalk that climbed up and up until it vanished into the clouds. Jack ran to the garden to take a closer look.

'I wonder where it ends?' thought Jack. 'I bet I could easily climb it and see!' So he took a firm hold and began to climb, *higher* and *higher* into the sky.

At the top, he found himself beside a cobbled road that led to an enormous castle. Jack stood still with his mouth gaping open – he couldn't believe his luck!

'You there, *stop*!' Jack turned and saw a woman rushing towards him. 'Do not go near that castle! A **monstrous giant** lives there who has stolen many treasures from the folk who live in this land. He eats children like you for breakfast!'

Now, Jack wasn't the brightest boy in the world, and he had never been in a castle before. So he ignored the woman, and continued up the road.

When Jack arrived at the castle, he knocked on the door, and it was opened by the **biggest**, **tallest** woman Jack had ever seen. She was, in fact, a giantess.

Jack cleared his throat. 'Good morning ma'am,' he said politely. 'Would you be so kind as to spare a poor boy some breakfast?'

The giantess had always liked children, so Jack was soon sitting at her table eating porridge out of one of her thimbles. Just as he finished his last spoonful, the house began to *shake*.

'Oh, *no!*' cried the giantess. 'My husband is home, and if he finds you here, he'll eat you for breakfast. **QUICK,** hide in the oven!'

Before Jack could think about whether or not an oven was the best place to hide from a hungry giant, he leapt in and the door was shut behind him.

The giant thumped into the room and stopped abruptly, sniffing the air. Then he cried out in a voice like thunder:

Fee-fi-fo-fum

I smell the blood of an Englishman!

Be he alive or be he dead,

I'll **grind his bones** to make my bread.

'Nonsense,' said the giantess. 'It must be the man you had for dinner yesterday.' She brought him a plate of roast beef, and patted his giant head.

Once the giant had finished his meal, he got up and opened the door to an adjoining room. Jack could see, through a crack in the oven door, that the room was filled with bags of glorious, **shining** gold. The giant sat down and began to count some of the money, until eventually his head began to nod and he started to snore.

Jack crept out of the oven. As he tiptoed past the giant, he snatched a bag of gold and ran as *fast* as he could to the beanstalk. When he got home, he told his mother of his adventure and proudly showed her his loot.

'With this money we can eat well for months!' she exclaimed.
She hugged Jack tightly.

Encouraged by his mother's reaction, Jack woke the next morning and climbed the beanstalk again. Once he reached the top, he ran past the woman (as she tried, again, to warn the silly boy), went straight to the castle door and knocked.

Soon Jack was sitting at the table, while the giantess smiled and watched him eat his porridge. But again, as he finished his breakfast, the house began to tremble. Jack quickly scrambled into the oven, just as the giant stomped in. The giant bellowed:

Fee-fi-fo-fum
I smell the blood of an Englishman!

Be he alive or be he dead,

I'll grind his bones

to make my bread.

But the giantess just chuckled
and gave the giant some
chicken nuggets.

Afterwards, the giant left the kitchen for a moment and came back holding a hen. The giant placed the hen and her nest on the table and said, 'LAY.'

Miraculously, the hen did as she was told and laid an egg made entirely of gold. After patting the hen and smiling at the egg for quite some time, the giant's head began to nod and he started to snore.

SNOORRRE

Quick as a flash, Jack crept out of the oven, grabbed hold of the hen and the golden egg, and climbed as fast as he could down the beanstalk.

When he got home, he proudly showed his mother the giant hen and she marvelled at the magnificent, **solid-gold** egg.

The next morning Jack was up the beanstalk before the sun had risen.

Once again, as Jack was eating porridge, the house began to *shake* and Jack climbed into the oven. The giant came in, bellowed something about an Englishman and ate his lamb wrap.

Then he got up and left the room for a moment, returning with a beautiful antique harp.

The giant put the harp on the table and said, *'Sing!'* At once, the golden harp came to life and began to sing beautifully. It sang until the giant's head began to nod and he began to snore.

Master, Master!

Jack crept out of the oven and snatched the harp from in front of the sleeping giant. But as he did, the harp cried out, 'Master, Master!' and the giant instantly awoke.

Jack ran as fast as he could back to the beanstalk, with the giant close behind. He scrambled down quickly and when he reached the bottom, his mother grabbed an axe and hacked at the beanstalk until it came tumbling down. The terrifying giant came crashing down with it, never to eat any Englishmen or steal from anyone ever again.

Scared out of his wits, Jack promised his mother that he would never make silly market deals again.

But one day, on his way to the market to sell his golden eggs and show his golden harp, Jack met a strange old man who made him an irresistible offer. And, in exchange for his hen and his harp, Jack became the proud owner of a horse that the old man assured him could fly.

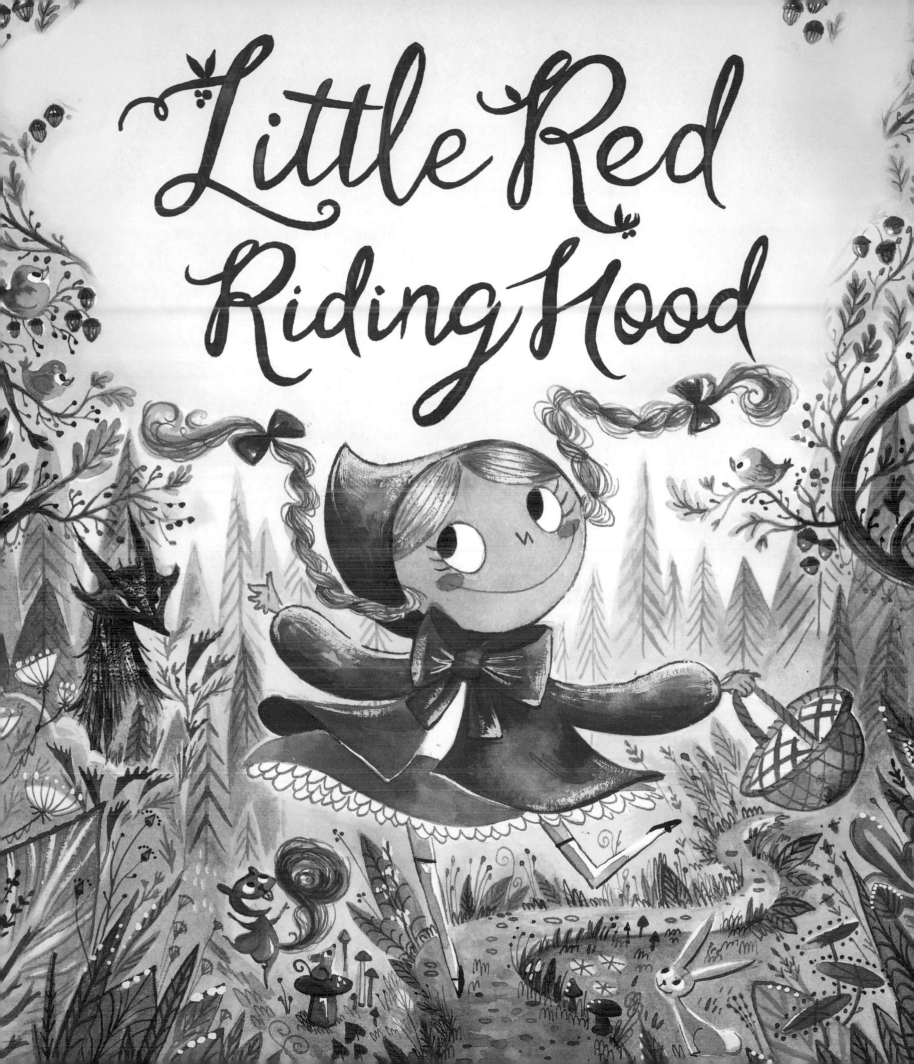

Once upon a time there lived a girl named Little Red Riding Hood. She was called that because she loved to wear a hooded cape of red velvet that her Grandmother had made for her.

One day, her mother said, 'Little Red Riding Hood, your poor Grandma is ill and you must take her this home-made pie.'

So Little Red Riding Hood pulled on her cape, placed the pie in her basket and sang merrily as she slipped out the door.

'Remember to stay on the path and *go straight there*,' called her mother as she left.

Little Red sighed, rolling her eyes. 'Mother is always giving me rules', she told the trees and the animals as she *skipped* down the path to Grandma's.

'**Don't** talk to strangers...
Don't wander into the woods...
Don't stick your finger in an ant's nest...'

Just at that moment, Little Red Riding Hood saw a patch of wildflowers that had sprung up in the woodland. She left the path and ran into the woods to gather up a handful of the beautiful blooms.

Little did Little Red know that a **hungry** Wolf was hiding behind a nearby tree, licking his lips as he imagined what a tasty snack the little girl would make. But he didn't dare make a meal of her here while he could hear the sound of woodcutters close by.

'How Granny will love these fragrant flowers,' she babbled away merrily as she picked.

'By golly that girl is a chatterbox,' thought the Wolf, as he hastily hatched his plan. 'But I bet she's **full** of flavour!' With that, he dashed off through the woods to Grandma's house.

When the Wolf arrived at Grandma's house, he rapped on the door and said, 'Grandma, Grandma, let me come in.'

But when Grandma replied, 'Not by the hair on my **chinny chin chin,**' the Wolf snapped his fingers in disappointment. That trick had not worked on those three pesky pigs either.

He needed a new plan.

This time he tapped lightly on the door, and, in his best little girl's voice said, 'Granny, it is I, Red Riding Hood. I've brought you some fine flowers to brighten up your room.'

'Oh, dear child,' replied Grandma, 'come right in, the door is unlocked.'

The Wolf opened the door, leapt inside and gobbled up Grandma in one mouthful!

Then he put on a set of her nightclothes and a nightcap, drew the curtains so that the room was quite dark, and lay down in her bed.

Little Red Riding Hood gathered a *lovely* posy of flowers and continued on her way to Grandmother's house. When she arrived, she knocked on the door. A husky voice called out, 'Who is there?'

'Little Red Riding Hood, with some tasty pie to make you feel better,' she replied.

'Come in,' called the Wolf. 'I am too weak to come to the door.'

So Little Red Riding Hood opened the door and went inside.

It was quite **dark** inside the house, but Little Red could see Grandma under the bedcovers, her nightcap pulled low over her face.

'Put the pie down and come say hello to your Grandma,' said the Wolf.

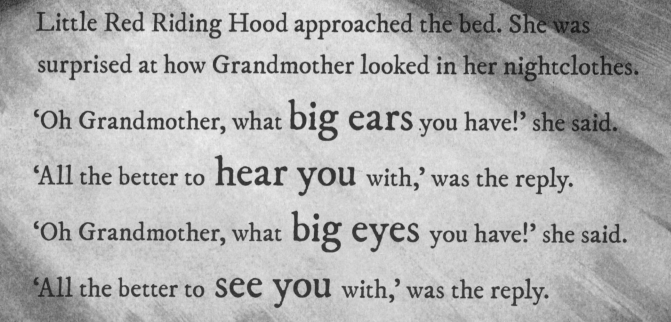

Little Red Riding Hood approached the bed. She was surprised at how Grandmother looked in her nightclothes.

'Oh Grandmother, what **big ears** you have!' she said.

'All the better to **hear you** with,' was the reply.

'Oh Grandmother, what **big eyes** you have!' she said.

'All the better to **see you** with,' was the reply.

'Oh Grandmother, what **big teeth** you have!' she said.

'All the better to eat you with!' replied the Wolf as he bounded out of bed and gulped down Little Red Riding Hood in one delicious mouthful.

GULP!

The Wolf felt sleepy after his big feast, and very comfortable in his new nightdress, so he lay down again in the bed and fell asleep. He started to snore very loudly.

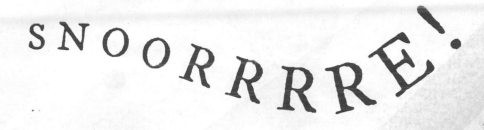

SNOORRRRE!

Just then, a woodcutter who lived nearby passed the house.

'Goodness, old Grandma is **snoring** even louder than usual,' he thought. 'I'd better see if she is all right.'

The woodcutter opened the door, peeked inside, and saw the Wolf lying fast asleep in Grandma's bed, his belly full. He *crept* up beside the Wolf but stopped as he heard an unusual sound over the Wolf's snoring.

He leaned his ear closer to the Wolf's bulging stomach and listened, and sure enough, he heard it clearly... it was the sound of a little girl chattering away.

He was able to guess what the wily Wolf had done.

The woodcutter leaped onto the bed and tackled the sleeping Wolf, who awoke with quite a fright.

The woodcutter seized the Wolf around the belly. He squeezed and he squeezed until the Wolf coughed and spluttered, and out popped Little Red Riding Hood! Then he **squeezed** and **squeezed** until the Wolf choked and sputtered, and out popped Grandma!

'Away with you,' cried the woodcutter to the Wolf, 'before I make a nice warm rug from your fur!' And the terrified Wolf fled into the wood, never to be seen again.

Little Red Riding Hood was so relieved at being freed that she made a vow to Grandma that she would never again break her Mother's rules.

But, on her way home that evening, Little Red Riding Hood found an ant's nest that was just **_too tempting_** to resist.

Once upon a time there lived a poor woodcutter, his wife, and his two children named Hansel and Gretel.

Though the woodcutter loved his children very much, his **wicked wife** wished them gone. There was a great famine throughout the land and she did not want to share what little food they had with her two *lousy* stepchildren.

One night, as the woodcutter worried over how he would feed his family, his wife told him, 'Do not worry, husband, for I have found some work for the children and myself at a house on the other side of the forest. I will take the children tomorrow and we will bring home a fine dinner.'

But Hansel, who lay awake in his bed, overheard this. He remembered the time that his stepmother had tried to sell him to a peddler in exchange for a new hat, and the time that she had tricked him into believing a nearby beehive was empty. He knew **she was up to no good.**

So the next morning, before they set out, Hansel filled his pockets with small brown pebbles from the garden.

As his stepmother led them through the forest, Hansel sprinkled a pebble here and a pebble there, creating a trail he could easily follow back home.

After many miles, Hansel and Gretel's stepmother turned to them and said, 'You poor children look thirsty. Wait here and I will fetch some water for you,' and she disappeared into the woods.

After some time, Hansel realised that he and his sister were stranded. Gretel began to cry, as little sisters often do. **'Fear not,'** said Hansel. **'I know the way.'** And they followed the path of pebbles home.

Hansel and Gretel arrived to find their father beside himself with worry. 'Your stepmother told me how you became separated. I thought you were lost **forever!**' he cried, pulling them both into a *fierce* hug.

Their stepmother, though really quite furious, pretended to be relieved. 'We shall set out **again** tomorrow,' she sighed, 'but this time we will make sure **everything** goes to plan.'

The following morning, Hansel and Gretel's stepmother woke them *very* early. She handed them each a piece of bread as their breakfast, and led them into the forest.

Hansel, having had no time to collect pebbles, but certain of what his stepmother was planning, broke the bread into little pieces and left a *trail of breadcrumbs* on the ground as they walked.

This time, their stepmother led them into a *deeper* part of the forest. After a long time, Gretel's legs became tired from walking so they all decided to rest by the trunk of a big tree. The children soon fell asleep.

When they awoke, it was **dark** and their stepmother was gone. Hansel built a small fire to keep them warm and told Gretel he would lead them home in the morning.

When daylight came, they set off along the path they had travelled the day before, but the breadcrumbs had disappeared. Hansel soon realised that the forest animals must have eaten them. 'Well, *that* was a **stupid idea**', he thought. They were totally and utterly lost. Gretel began to cry.

At that moment, they heard a *sweet song* coming from a nearby tree. Looking around in surprise, Gretel saw a snow white bird sitting on a low branch and swallowed her tears to watch it. When the bird flitted out of the tree and into the forest, Gretel ran after it, and Hansel followed close behind. The beautiful bird led them to a clearing in the forest.

Standing in the middle of the clearing was a beautiful cottage made from gingerbread, and *covered in sweets*. It was the most exquisite thing Hansel and Gretel had ever seen.

The children ran to the cottage and began taking bites from the gingerbread door, pulling off parts of the sweet-covered walls and licking the clear toffee windows.

As they were eating, they heard a soft voice call from inside the house:

'Nibble, nibble, **little** mouse,

Who is nibbling at **my** house?'

Suddenly the door opened and a very old woman came hobbling out. Hansel and Gretel were terribly frightened at first, but the old woman seemed very kind.

'You poor children,' she said, 'You must be starving, come inside and sit by the fire while I make you a **hearty** meal.' She prepared dinner for Hansel and Gretel, and set up two soft beds with thick, warm blankets. The children ate hungrily and then fell fast asleep.

Little did Hansel and Gretel know that although the old woman had been kind to the children, she was actually a *wicked witch* who liked to eat little boys!

The next morning, while he was still half asleep, the witch seized Hansel and forced him into a cage. **'You will make a pretty mouthful!'** she cackled.

In the following weeks, the witch cooked Hansel all the food he could eat and made Gretel her servant. Because she had terrible eyesight, each morning the witch would make Hansel poke one finger out of the cage so that she could feel how he was fattening up.

But Hansel, being the clever boy he was, had kept a chicken bone from one of his meals and each day he would poke it out of the cage for the witch to feel. She could not understand why he wasn't becoming **plump** and *juicy*!

One day, fed up with waiting for Hansel to fatten up into a *delicious* roast, the witch decided instead to make him into a lovely stew. She made Gretel fetch water and boil it in a big pot with lots of vegetables. The witch sat by cackling cheerfully and rubbing her hands together.

While the stock for the stew was boiling away, the witch
ordered Gretel to help her bake some bread.

Gretel kneaded the dough then gave the loaf to the witch,
who leaned into the oven to place the bread inside.

Gretel saw her chance – she quickly shoved the
witch into the oven and *slammed* the
door closed!

'You saved my life!'
Hansel cried, very proud of
his brave sister. Gretel quickly
unlocked Hansel's cage and
set him free.

Quickly, Hansel and Gretel both found large sacks and ran around the house filling them with as much food as they could carry. Gretel also took a large jar of tasty-looking rock candy. They set out into the woods again, *determined* to find their way home.

After wandering through the woods for another day and night, Hansel finally began to recognise the forest around him. Though Gretel was exhausted, both children began to run when they saw the first glimpse of their home through the forest trees.

Their father heard their hurried footsteps and came rushing out the door, sweeping both children into his arms as soon as he saw them. **'I've searched high and low for you!'** he cried. 'When your stepmother told me she had lost you both, I was wild with worry. When she refused to help find you I quickly realised her treachery and sent her away. **We will never have to see her again!'**

Inside the house, Hansel and Gretel emptied their sacks and their father was relieved to see there would be enough food to get them through the coming winter. But when Gretel pulled out her jar of rock candy, her father exclaimed. For it turned out that this was not rock candy after all, but precious gems worth a *great fortune*!

So they all lived happily ever after... but Hansel and Gretel never ate sweets again.

There once lived a rich merchant who had three beautiful daughters. One winter's day, as the merchant was about to set off upon a long journey, he asked his daughters, 'What gifts would you like me to bring you when I return?'

As expected, the two eldest asked for silk gowns and jewels.
But when his youngest daughter, Beauty, asked only for his safe return, the merchant insisted that she choose a gift as a reward for being such a loving daughter.

Beauty thought for a moment and said, 'I would be so grateful if you could bring me a single rose. I do love them so.'

Several weeks later, as the merchant was travelling home, the sky turned **dark** and snow began to fall, freezing him to the bone. Chilling winds swept the land and the merchant knew he must find shelter or perish.

Finally, he saw some lights shining in the distance. Cold and shivering, he made his way along the road until he reached a majestic castle.

Much to his surprise, the merchant found one of the castle doors open. Through the door he could see the warm glow of a hearty fire, and was drawn inside. He called out as he entered, but there was no reply.

Once inside, the merchant found a long dining table set for one. He hesitantly sat down but soon started feasting on hot stew, roasted duck and vegetables. Then the merchant sat in a big chair beside the fire and soon fell fast asleep.

The next morning, the merchant awoke to find a warm blanket draped over him and a fine suit laid out for him to wear. On the dining table was a magnificent breakfast for one.

The merchant ate his breakfast, dressed in the suit, and called out a *'thank-you!'* to whatever magical being had taken him in for the night. As he went outside to fetch his horse, the merchant noticed a gate leading to a garden.

Remembering Beauty's request, he entered the garden to find row upon row of blossoming roses. He chose a perfect pink bloom, and tore it from the bush.

Suddenly there was a great howl, and the merchant looked up to see a terrible creature rushing towards him.

'How *dare* you!' yelled the Beast. 'I have given you everything you could need, and still you steal from me.'

The merchant felt both scared and sorry. 'Please forgive me,' he begged, 'I only took the rose for my daughter, who loves them so.'

But the Beast would not forgive him so easily. The following morning, he sent the merchant home with a horrible demand. The merchant feared the Beast's punishment if he did not do as he was told, and left the castle with a **heavy** heart.

When the merchant arrived home, he told his daughters what had transpired on his journey. With great regret, he repeated the Beast's demand. 'One of you must go to live with the Beast of your own free will,' he said sadly, 'or I am doomed.'

'*I* will go, Papa,' said Beauty. The merchant was distraught at the idea, but Beauty wouldn't have it any other way. So, one week later, they set out for the Beast's castle.

When they arrived at the castle, Beauty was awed by its charm. Again, the door was open and the table was set with a wonderful feast.

As they finished their meal, a terrible **ROAR** came from the top of the stairs and the Beast appeared. Beauty was terrified of the hideous creature, but was determined not to let her father down.

The Beast asked if she had come willingly, and Beauty bravely replied, 'Yes.'

'I am pleased,' growled the Beast.

The next morning, after her father tearfully departed, Beauty sat upon the steps, weeping. After a time though, she became curious and began to explore the castle. Upstairs, she found a room with her name on the door.

Inside, there were fine furnishings, clothes, jewels, books and even a harp. Beauty soon understood that she would want for nothing while this was her home.

That night, as Beauty went down to dinner, the Beast met her on the stairway. 'May I join you?' he asked in his **gruff**, *growly* voice.

'Of course,' replied Beauty. 'This is your home after all.'

During the meal, Beauty found that the Beast was surprisingly well-mannered.

Afterwards, the Beast asked Beauty, 'Will you marry me?' Beauty simply shook her head.

The following months passed quickly. Beauty spent her days exploring the castle and wandering in the garden.

Every night she talked and laughed with the Beast over dinner. Beauty soon found that these meals were the best parts of her day.

But, at the end of each evening, when the Beast would ask Beauty to marry him, Beauty would sadly tell him no.

'Beast, you are my *dearest* friend,' she told him one night. 'Can't you be happy with that?'

'I love you with all of my heart,' said the Beast, 'But I can only be happy if you promise to stay here forever!'

Beauty was happy at the castle, but she missed her father; so she made a deal with the Beast. 'If you permit me to go home to my family for one month, I will return to the castle forever', she said.

'Please come back to me, Beauty,' the Beast said. '**I cannot live without you.**'

The next day, Beauty returned home to her father, who had become ill with worry. He was very glad to have her home and soon returned to full health.

Time passed by so quickly that Beauty barely noticed when a month had passed. Then one night she had a terrible dream where she saw the Beast lying in the garden, gravely ill. The next morning she travelled back to the castle as quickly as she could.

When she arrived, she searched the castle but could find no sign of the Beast. Terrified, she ran to the garden, where she found him lying on the ground – she rushed to his side.

'I'm sorry I was gone so long,' Beauty whispered, 'I didn't realise how much I loved you until it was too late. *I will marry you*, Beast, if you'll just wake up!'

Then, a miraculous thing happened. The Beast began to shake, and soon there was no longer a creature lying before Beauty, but a handsome prince.

Beauty was shocked and asked where her Beast had gone, but the prince replied, 'I am right here!' He told Beauty how an evil witch had cast a spell on him that could only be broken by *true love*.

Beauty and the prince were married the next day. A grand carriage was sent to fetch Beauty's father and sisters, and the king and queen soon arrived to attend the wedding.

The king and queen were so grateful to Beauty for breaking their son's curse that they made her father a great lord, and they all lived *happily ever after*.

NOTES FOR THE READER

PUSS IN BOOTS

The best-known version of 'Puss in Boots' was written by Frenchman Charles Perrault in 1697. It was included in *Contes de ma Mère l'Oye* (*Tales of my Mother Goose*), a collection of fairytales and stories.

It is thought that Perrault adapted his story from the earliest known recorded version of the tale called *Fortunato Costantino* ('Lucky Costantino') written by Italian writer Giovanni Franceso Straparola in his collection of stories from the 1550s, *Le Piacevoli Potti* (published in English as the *The Facetious Nights of Straparola*).

There are many variants of the 'Puss in Boots' story that can be found in different cultures around the world. Interestingly, the cat is not always male, with some stories seeing a female Puss take the lead. Animals other than cats are also cast in the helper role, such as a fox or a gazelle. In some versions, the cat is actually a fairy in disguise or a woman who has been bewitched, who ends up marrying her master once the spell has been removed.

Another common variation has the cat testing its owner's gratitude by pretending to be dead or dangerously ill. In these versions the owner promises the cat a burial in a golden coffin when it dies. However, when the owner refuses to provide treatment for the sick cat or orders the supposedly dead cat's body be thrown on a dung heap or down a well, the cat either angrily takes its leave or reveals the humble origins of its owner. Perrault opted for a much happier ending for the cat and owner, with both becoming members of the nobility and leading lives of leisure.

SNOW WHITE AND THE SEVEN DWARFS

The story of 'Snow White' was told in many versions from Europe, Asia and Africa since the Middle Ages, passed down through word-of-mouth over the centuries before the Brothers Grimm recorded it in *Kinder- und Hausmärchen* (*Children's and Household Tales*) in 1810.

Some traditional versions of the story have Snow White rescued by robbers instead of dwarfs. Instead of a magic mirror, the stepmother converses with the sun or moon, or sometimes an animal.

The Brothers Grimm changed 'Snow White' quite dramatically from their initial manuscript to the final published version of the tale that we are familiar with today. Initially, it was Snow White's own mother who tried to kill her, not her stepmother. Her mother takes her into the woods to gather flowers, then abandons her. At the end of the story, the king has his wife executed. It is thought this was changed by the Brothers Grimm to make the story more suitable for children at the time.

In the final version of the Grimms' story, the evil stepmother eats the heart that the hunter gives her as proof of Snow White's death. She also attends the wedding, where the prince forces her to dance wearing red-hot iron shoes until she falls down dead. Modern versions of the story have Snow White awakened with a kiss, instead of the apple falling from her throat.

JACK AND THE BEANSTALK

The story of Jack's adventures on the beanstalk is a very old one, and there are many different versions. It began as an oral tale, possibly more than 5,000 years ago. The first literary version was published in the second edition of *Round About Our Coal-Fire* in 1734 as 'The Story of Jack Spriggins and the Enchanted Bean'. In 1807, Benjamin Tabart published *The History of Jack and the Bean Stalk*, which contained many moralistic elements that were probably created by Tabart rather than taken from the oral tale. The version most commonly used in fairy tale collections to this day is that of Joseph Jacobs, published in *English Fairy Tales* in 1890, which is considered by many to be closer to the original oral version.

The most popular versions of the story, including the one in this collection, portray the characters involved in vastly different ways. It is thought that the original story doesn't involve giants at all, and has Jack behaving decidedly badly – he courts another man's wife, hides in his house, and eventually robs and kills him. Benjamin Tabart's 1807 retelling adjusts the story to make Jack more sympathetic – a fairy woman reveals to Jack that the giant robbed and killed his father, justifying Jack's actions as revenge or retribution for the giant's misdeeds. The story in this collection portrays Jack as an innocent hero and the giant as a terrifying menace to the local villagers. Other variants, such as Stephen Sondheim's musical *Into the Woods* or Brian Henson's television miniseries *Jack and the Beanstalk: The Real Story*, show the giant and his wife as misunderstood and unfairly treated by Jack and the villagers.

LITTLE RED RIDING HOOD

Like many fairytales, the first versions of 'Little Red Riding Hood' were told aloud and rarely written down, but they were popular all around the world. The story of *La Finta Nonna* ('The False Grandmother') was shared by Italian peasants in the fourteenth century, and the Chinese story of 'Grandaunt Tiger' is still told today in Taiwan by the descendants of families who immigrated from mainland China.

The most famous versions of this tale are Charles Perrault's *Le Petit Chaperon Rouge* ('Little Red Riding Hood'), published in 1697, and 'Rotkäppchen', collected and published by the Brothers Grimm in 1812 and revised in 1857. Perrault's tale is probably the first to introduce the titular red hood, and many regard it as much darker and more moralised than other versions. This story ends with Red Riding Hood being eaten by the wolf, and contains an explicit warning to young children (especially young girls) not to talk to strangers, no matter how nice they might seem. In the version published by the Brothers Grimm in *Kinder- und Hausmärchen* (Children's and Household Tales), a happier ending is introduced – the little girl and her grandmother are saved by a huntsman after being swallowed by the wolf.

Another well-known variant, 'The True History of Little Goldenhood', was written by Andrew Lang in his 1890 collection, *The Red Fairy Book*, in which the little girl does not wear a red hood and is not eaten by the wolf or saved by the huntsman. She wears an enchanted golden hood, and this is what saves her from the wolf.

HANSEL AND GRETEL

'Hansel and Gretel' was originally recorded by the Brothers Grimm. They heard it from Dortchen Wild, a storyteller who later married the younger Grimm brother, Wilhelm.

The Grimms first recorded 'Hansel and Gretel' in 1812, but there are differences between the original and the final edition of 1857. The most noticeable difference is the woman. In the original story, she is the children's mother. By the final version, she was changed to a stepmother, just like in their Snow White tale, to make the story more appropriate for children, reflecting the story's popularity within the conservative middle class. The characters Hansel and Gretel were originally named 'Little Brother' and 'Little Sister'. The Grimms chose the names Hansel and Gretel because they were so common; they are the German equivalents of John and Jane.

Stories about parents abandoning their children or children lost in the woods, such as 'The Babes in the Wood' and 'Baba Yaga', are common across many cultures. In medieval times, it was not unknown for parents to abandon their children when they could no longer feed them. In their introduction, the Grimms note several stories with similar themes. In one, it is a wolf, not a witch, who lives in the house. In another, three princesses follow a thread, then a trail of ashes and finally peas, which are eaten by pigeons.

In 1893, 'Hansel and Gretel' was turned into an opera by the German composer Engelbert Humperdinck. The opera became hugely popular and helped make the story as well-known as it is today.

BEAUTY AND THE BEAST

Versions of the *Beauty and the Beast* story have been told for centuries. For instance, an ancient Roman myth called *Cupid and Psyche* features a beautiful maiden cursed by the goddess Venus to fall in love with a snake. However, Venus's son Cupid falls in love with Psyche and turns himself into the serpent, before revealing himself as a young man at the end of the tale. The story of a beautiful girl caring for a beast, only to have him turn into a man, is found throughout many tales from Asia and Europe.

Other early European versions of the story include *The Pig King* by Italian Giovanni Straparola, published in *Piacevoli Potti* (published in English as *The Facetious Nights of Straparola*) in 1550 with the beast as a pig, and the first version to be named *La Belle et la Bête* (*Beauty and the Beast*), written in 1650 by French aristocrat Marie-Catherine Le Jumel de Barneville and featuring a serpent beast.

In 1740, Madame Gabrielle-Suzanne Barbot de Gallon de Villeneuve wrote the first modern version of the tale. Her version of *Beauty and the Beast* was 362 pages long and featured fairies, kings and twelve brothers and sisters.

The version of 'Beauty and the Beast' most familiar to modern readers was published in 1756 by Madame Jeanne-Marie Le Prince de Beaumont, in a collection called *Magasin des enfants*. This version has the two jealous sisters marrying wealthy men, only to have unhappy marriages, while Beauty, who accepts the hideous but good Beast, ends up happy and content.